MARVELLA'S HOBBY

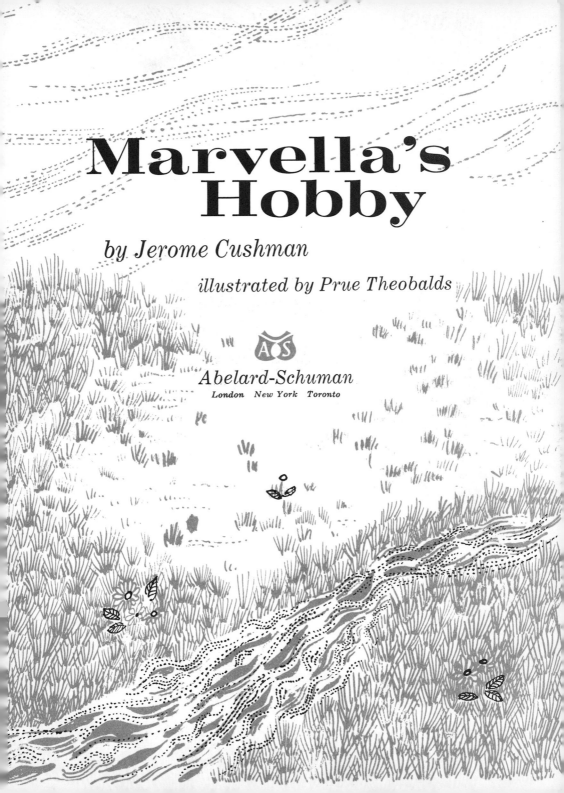

Marvella's Hobby

by Jerome Cushman

illustrated by Prue Theobalds

Abelard-Schuman

London   New York   Toronto

LONDON
Abelard-Schuman
Limited
8 King Street

NEW YORK
Abelard-Schuman
Limited
6 West 57th Street

TORONTO
Abelard-Schuman
Canada Limited
81 John Street

Printed in the United States of America

Dedicated to Debora and Sara Beth,
Marvella's first friends.

Marvella was a happy Brown Swiss cow. She lived on Mr. Howard's farm in Kansas.

Roly-poly Mr. Howard was so fond of Marvella that he had given her a pasture of her own. In summer this was paradise. The wind blew softly, the sun shone warmly, the grass grew tender and tall. A swift flowing brook flowed through the pasture, providing a cool drink whenever Marvella was thirsty. And a spreading elm tree provided shady rest. Summer in the pasture was the time Marvella liked best.

Afternoons there were for resting, but mornings

and evenings were for doing. For Marvella had a hobby. Her hobby was a train.

Every morning she went to the south corner of her pasture where the fence made a V. She stretched her neck over the fence and looked up the railroad track which curved alongside the field. She waited, sometimes ten minutes, sometimes an hour, for the sound she knew so well.

It always came—the faint "To-o-ot to-o-o-t" of the freight train Number 10 in the distance.

Marvella made ready. When the green and silver diesel engine rounded the gentle curve directly in front of Marvella, its whistle gave a mighty blast.

"Too-o-t too-o-t" sounded the whistle and the echo came back from the woods a quarter of a mile away.

Marvella took a deep breath.

"Moo-oo-oo" was her answer to the train whistle, and it meant, "Good morning." This completed her hobby work for the morning.

She then proceeded to the serious business of eating some of the tender grass, drinking cool water from the brook and resting in the comfortable shade of the elm tree.

When the evening shadows slowly moved across the pasture she walked to the south corner again and waited. This time, as she stretched her neck across the fence, she looked down the track. Faintly in the distance came the sound of the train whistle.

Soon the big green and silver engine came to Marvella's fence corner and its mighty "Too-oo-t too-oo-t" shook the leaves of the spreading elm tree.

Marvella took a deep breath and her "Moo-oo-oo" was mighty too. This time it meant "Good night."

Satisfied that she had done right by her hobby, she slowly walked up to the barn where Mr. Howard was waiting for her with a shiny milk pail in his hand.

"Did you have a good day, Marvella?" asked Mr. Howard.

He enjoyed talking to her. She seemed so under-

standing. As she looked at him with her sad gentle
eyes she often nodded her head, as if in agreement
with him.

"Marvella," he went on, "I've been meaning to
speak to you about one of your little habits.

17

"Every time old Number 10 goes past the farm you moo your heart out. Now don't deny it. The other morning you were bawling at the train engine like a calf.

"What a silly idea, Marvella! Serenading a train in broad daylight!" And he laughed at the idea until his cheeks were pink.

Marvella shook her head slowly from side to side. Some might say that she was brushing away flies, but Mr. Howard knew better. She was telling him she didn't agree with him.

Marvella wasn't really cross. She knew that gentle Mr. Howard was only having fun. After all, she said to herself proudly, it isn't every Brown Swiss cow that has a freight engine for a hobby.

After the milking Marvella noticed Mr. Howard scurrying about faster than usual. He seemed to be making sure that all the doors and windows of the barn were closed.

"Looks like big wind weather," Mr. Howard was muttering to himself. "You never can tell about

18

Kansas!" Even as he spoke the wind made a ghost-like howling noise around the corners of the barn. This made Mr. Howard hurry faster than ever.

"Good night, Marvella," he said as he closed the big barn door. "I've got to run to the house before it pours."

Marvella thought how funny roly-poly Mr. Howard would look running to the farmhouse. She just knew that, if necessary, she could run faster than her master.

It grew darker. The wind blew harder. It began

to rain. Marvella enjoyed the noise of the rain on the roof, although soon it was louder than she had ever remembered. But she did not like the sound of the wind. Its howl turned into a roar and its fury caused the whole barn to shake and rattle. Marvella half expected the barn to tumble down any moment.

She was angry at the wind because it kept her from dreaming about her engine. In fact she couldn't even sleep, for she had a feeling something dreadful might happen if she did.

When the first glimmer of daylight brought Mr.

Howard for the morning milking she mooed with welcome relief. As usual, he told Marvella the latest radio news.

"It was a first class big wind, Marvella. But we only got the tail end of the storm. The tornado struck twenty miles up the line. It caused a lot of damage."

Marvella listened to Mr. Howard's account of the news, but not too intently. She wanted to go to her pasture. Storm or no storm, she had no intention of neglecting her train. She felt it needed her—especially today.

When Marvella went out, she found the barnyard filled with water—it was almost a lake! But the sun was coming up over the treetops. The day would be fair.

Marvella hurried to her pasture, took her place in the south corner where the fence made a V, and waited. She waited until her legs grew tired, but the train did not come.

The sun grew warm. She wanted a cool drink of

water and a lunch of tender grass and a rest in the
shade. But she did not stir from the south corner
where the fence made a V.

From time to time, she stretched her head over
the fence and looked anxiously first up and then
down the track. And she listened—listened for the
sound of her train whistle. There was no sound.
There was no train.

All day she stood by the fence. Her head drooped
lower and lower. When the shadows of evening
spread over her pasture she was still there—waiting.

It was milking time. Mr. Howard, shiny pail in his

hand, waited for Marvella to come up to the barn. She did not come. Mr. Howard became a little impatient.

"It isn't like Marvella to forget milking time. Perhaps she doesn't feel well. I'll just go to the pasture and have a look," he said to himself.

When he arrived, there was Marvella anxiously looking up and down the railroad track, nervously shifting from one foot to the other. She paid no attention to her master. Her eyes did not stray from the railroad track.

Mr. Howard went up to Marvella and in a cajoling voice said, "Marvella, it isn't like you to forget milking time. I do believe you must be sick."

Marvella turned her head towards Mr. Howard, glanced briefly at him, and then continued to gaze up and down the track.

This hurt Mr. Howard's feelings. He did not like being ignored by Marvella.

His voice had a tinge of anger as he said, "You're just being stubborn, Marvella. Now come up to the

barn and right now. Do you think I've got all night
for the milking?"

Marvella acted as if she did not hear him.

Mr. Howard could not believe his eyes. Was this
the gentle beautiful cow he had raised from a calf?
Was this the friend he had pampered and petted
and given a pasture of her very own? It was ingrati-
tude—that's what it was.

28

"Come, Marvella," he said, this time with real anger in his voice.

She did not even look around.

For the first time in his life, Mr. Howard lost his temper with Marvella. He struck her—on the back.

It was not a hard blow, but it took her by surprise. She gave him a shocked look. Could her old friend have done such a thing?

Suddenly she turned away from the fence and without another glance at Mr. Howard started toward the barn.

He followed her slowly, feeling guilty for losing his temper.

When he got to the barn she was waiting for him in her stall. He picked up his shiny pail and three-legged stool and, not daring to look at her sad, accusing eyes, started with the milking.

She did not co-operate. She moved restlessly from side to side, her head swaying back and forth. Her tail was most active. She seemed to be taking aim. With one flick she hit Mr. Howard on the head, knocking his hat off.

He started to protest and—flick—her tail got in his open mouth.

Mr. Howard worked hard but after twenty minutes there was barely enough milk to cover the bottom of the pail.

Then Marvella made her revenge complete. She calmly put her hind foot in the milk pail.

"Thunderation!" yelled Mr. Howard, his face red with anger.

"What has got into you? You're sick. I know it. I'm going to call Doc Anderson and have him come out and look at you in the morning. And Marvella, I will NOT wish you good night.

"Good night," Mr. Howard said, forgetting himself as he stamped angrily out of the barn.

Marvella did not seem to hear this last outburst of her master. Her purpose had been accomplished and she was now ready to give her attention to important things—like thinking about her train.

First she listened, but no "Too-oo-t too-oo-t" gladdened her heart. So she did the next best thing.

She thought about her train and thought about her train and thought about her train until she dreamed about her train and dreamed about her train and dreamed about her train all night long. And as her dream train blew its dream whistle, she mooed in her sleep.

She was awakened by the sound of voices and ap-
proaching footsteps.

The barn door let in the daylight, a worried Mr.
Howard, and a little man, carrying a black leather
bag.

"I'm fretful about Marvella, Andy. She just isn't herself," said Mr. Howard.

"We'll find out what's ailing her," answered Dr. Anderson, the veterinarian, in his best professional voice.

He was a short man and he moved about with quick hopping steps.

He patted Marvella on the neck and said "So-o-o-o Bossy, so-o-o."

It made Marvella nervous to be patted on the neck by strangers. And she didn't like being called Bossy.

"Take her over by the big door," ordered the doctor. "I need more light."

Mr. Howard went to Marvella, patted her and said, "Don't be afraid, Marvella. Ol' Andy Anderson will have you pert and snuffy in no time."

When Marvella looked through the open barn door, and saw the road just fifty feet away, a plan suddenly came to her mind.

The stubborn Marvella of yesterday was no more. Now she would co-operate. She pulled Mr. Howard along in her haste to get to the door.

Dr. Anderson prepared for the examination. "Now let me see," he said, still using his professional voice.

"I believe we ought to take Bossy's temperature. Eh, Bossy?"

Marvella snorted with displeasure.

"We'll just open this little black bag," he said, as he took the key out of his pocket.

He turned the key in the lock but the bag would not open. He pulled and pulled at it. The lock was stuck.

"Wouldn't you know it?" grunted Dr. Anderson, as he jerked the bag this way and that.

"Let me help you," offered Mr. Howard.

This fitted in perfectly with Marvella's plan—her plan to escape.

While Dr. Anderson and Mr. Howard struggled with the black bag, Marvella simply walked out of the big barn door.

Once she was outside she quickly walked over to the road. Then with a glance at the barn to see if she was being followed, she started up the road at an ungainly gallop.

The two men were so intent upon opening the doctor's black bag that they did not notice her absence.

After much grunting and groaning the men jerked
the bag open, spilling medicine all over the floor.

"Now, Marvella," said Mr. Howard, "the doctor
will take your . . . She's gone!" he exclaimed.

He ran out of the barn, followed by Dr. Anderson.
They were just in time to see Marvella lumbering
along in the direction of Jackman's Corner where

the railroad tracks crossed the road.

"Marvella," yelled Mr. Howard. "Wait!"

The two men ran after her, their short legs churning the muddy road.

Mr. Howard resembled a bear running on his hind legs.

Dr. Anderson ran like a chicken.

41

Marvella was too far away to hear the cries of the men but even so, she would not have stopped. Her mind was made up. She knew what she must do.

Quiet, easy-going Marvella was now a Brown Swiss cow with a purpose. She would find her train no matter how long the road.

She reached Jackman's Corner and the railroad tracks.

Here she rested a moment, looking back to see if the two men were gaining on her. But they were tiny specks in the distance.

They were resting, too.

With only a moment's hesitation, she turned to the right and began to walk in the middle of the track.

The cinders hurt her feet but she did not care. Marvella settled down to an easy trot, her eyes intent on the track ahead.

Although she became tired she did not stop. And she kept listening, listening for her beloved train whistle.

Instead, a strange sound came to her ears, a rustling, swirling sound. She knew it was water, probably "her" brook.

Yet it did not sound like "her" brook.

Soon she saw it, muddy angry water flowing swiftly down the hill to join Dry Creek. Only the creek wasn't dry—it was filled by the rain that had fallen during the storm.

There was a bridge over the creek.

But it was not like any bridge that Marvella had ever seen.

It was tilted at a crazy angle. One end of the bridge was in the water and of course the track was in the water too.

Marvella stopped at the edge of the bridge, wondering what to do.

She must get to the other side. Nothing would stop her.

She made her way to the muddy riverbank and started down. But it was so steep and slippery that she slid most of the way.

The water was cold and swift but not too deep.

Marvella walked bravely to the other side, holding her head high until she felt dry ground under her feet. Then she scrambled up that bank and struggled through some underbrush until she reached the middle of the railroad track, where it started up again after the bridge.

Marvella was very tired and she sat down to rest.

Then it happened.

She could hardly believe her ears.

A train whistle—her train whistle—sounded far in the distance.

Faintly she heard the familiar "To-o-o-t Too-oo-t."
Then it came louder and louder.

She saw the train just as it rounded a gentle curve.
It headed straight for Marvella.

Marvella remembered the bridge in the water.
Her train was in danger!

She must do something.

She stood up, took a deep breath and let forth
with a mighty "Moo-oo-oo!"

Mr. Wright, the engineer, was thinking of the rain,
and how a flooded stretch of track had brought the
train to a halt. He had a great deal of time to make
up now, and a cow was the furthest thing from his
mind.

Mr. Wright, however, was a prudent engineer,
and as prudent engineers do, he looked out of his cab
at the track ahead. His heart almost jumped flip-flop.

"Cow on the track!" he shouted to the fireman.
"Hold on!"

He pulled the brake lever back with both hands,

as hard as he could. The freight cars clattered and
the brakes screamed.

But the train kept coming closer and closer to
Marvella.

Marvella did not move an inch. Defiantly, she held her head high.

The train grew larger and larger, nearer and nearer. The brakes screamed even more loudly. But Marvella was not afraid.

Finally with a bumping and thumping all along the line of freight cars, the train stopped—less than

twelve inches from Marvella's nose.

Engineer Wright was angry. He and Fireman
Vander came down from the cab.

"I wonder who this consarned cow belongs to,"
shouted Mr. Wright. "Don't people know there's a
law against cows on railroad property?"

"Look!" said Fireman Vander in a frightened voice.

Mr. Wright turned around, and only then did he see the broken bridge. He turned white with fear and then red with embarrassment.

"Well, I'll be!" he said. "This cow saved the train from a terrible wreck."

"MAR—VELLA!" called Mr. Howard. In a few moments Mr. Howard and Dr. Anderson were on the other side of the bridge, both hot and tired.

"How did you get over there, Marvella?" shouted Mr. Wright.

"Look," said Dr. Anderson. "She slid down the bank and waded over."

"I suppose we must too," said Mr. Howard.

So both of them slid down the muddy bank like otters, waded across Dry Creek, and soon were on the track with Marvella, the engineer and the fireman.

"My name is Wright," said the engineer as he shook hands with Mr. Howard and Dr. Anderson. "And this is Paul Vander, my fireman."

"Glad to meet you," said Mr. Howard. "This cow

of mine has been a mite of trouble for the last day or so."

Marvella paid no attention to the conversation. She was looking lovingly at the big green and silver engine, mooing softly, and switching her tail slowly from side to side.

The engineer said, "My name is Wright and I know I'm *right*. I've seen this cow somewhere before."

"Of course you have," answered Mr. Howard.

"Marvella moos to you every morning and evening. Her day is not complete unless she can say 'Howdy' to the train. Your train is Marvella's hobby."

"By golly," exclaimed Dr. Anderson, who had been looking Marvella over, "I believed she's cured! She was just lonesome for her train, that's all. She will be all right now. I'll stake my professional reputation on it."

"Seems like we ought to reward Marvella for saving the train," said Fireman Vander.

"A fine idea," chimed in Mr. Wright. He took off

the striped bandanna handkerchief from around his neck and tied it into a pretty bow on Marvella's right horn.

"I appoint you Special Engineer of Train Number 10," he said.

Mr. Vander tied his polka dot bandanna in a pretty bow on Marvella's left horn.

"I appoint you Special Fireman of Train Number 10," he added.

Marvella was proud. One could see that, no matter how modest she tried to appear.

"Come, Marvella, it is time for us to go home," said Mr. Howard.

"Will we have to slide down the mud bank and cross Dry Creek again?" anxiously asked Dr. Anderson.

"That's the way to get to the other side," replied Mr. Howard. "So let's have fun doing it."

He ran over to the steep mud bank and shouted, "Whe-e-e" all the way down.

Dr. Anderson went down belly-whopper just for fun.

But Marvella, very dignified, sat down and carefully slid into the water.

Then all three of them waded Dry Creek and started for home. The men waved good-bye to their new friends across the bridge, and Marvella gave one last loving look at green and silver Engine Number 10.

Every morning, Marvella waits in the south corner of her pasture where the fence makes a V.

When Train Number 10 rounds the curve in front of the Howard farm it goes, "Too-oo-ooot Too-oo-oo-t." Marvella goes "Moo-ooo-oo" which means "Good morning."

When there are shadows on the pasture and the sun begins to sink behind the grove of trees, Train Number 10 comes back, on its way to the roundhouse.

"Too-oo-oo-t, Too-oo-oo-t" it whistles as it passes Marvella.

Marvella, Special Engineer and Fireman of Train Number 10, answers, "Moo-oo Moo-oo" which means, "Good night."